W9-DJP-033

yellow

# THE
# SLEEPERS

## ALF NUSSMAN

**Fearon**
Belmont, California

**DOUBLE FASTBACK® MYSTERY Books**

Cover photographer: Richard Hutchings

ISBN 0–8224–2366–9

Library of Congress Catalog Card Number: 86–81007

Printed in the United States of America

1. 9 8 7 6 5 4 3 2 1

$B$illy Mason limped out of his doctor's office with his right ankle taped. He used a single crutch to help keep his weight off the sprain, but it still hurt.

The doctor had said he'd be as good as new in a couple of weeks. Until then, Billy should try to stay off the ankle.

That was easy for the doctor to say. His customers came to him. Billy, on the other hand, had to go out and get his customers. Every day he spent at home meant the possibility of losing valuable contacts. He had to make the rounds of agents' offices, talk to performers, keep his face in view. How else could he know who needed material and what kind? Comedians don't advertise in the newspapers. They like people to think they write their own jokes.

Everyone called Mason "Billy." You'd think a 30-year-old man would be a William, not a Billy, but he *looked* like a Billy. He was short, hardly five feet seven. He had a slim body and a round, boyish face. His curly blond hair always seemed to be hanging in his eyes. He had a high-pitched voice and a nervous manner. When he acted out a routine he was trying to sell, he'd jump around and wave his arms. It was as if he were describing a dogfight between two fighter planes.

Sometimes he had to show proof of his age before he could get into nightclubs to see his own jokes performed. People told true stories about him that were as funny as any he made up and sold. He was a Billy.

As he made his way down the street, Billy felt sure he had been cursed. Somewhere in Manhattan a witch doctor was sticking pins into a straw doll that looked like him. He would bet money on it. How else could he explain the run of bad luck that had dogged him? His job with the Letterman show had fallen through before he'd even gotten it. No one had called him in weeks. And now he'd gotten this twisted ankle.

All he needed now was to be mugged for the money he didn't have in his pocket. That would top it all off nicely. If he had known that he would also soon be involved in a mystery and two suspicious deaths, he wouldn't have been surprised. Frightened, yes; surprised, no.

He had traveled the five blocks from the doctor's office to the subway entrance without getting pushed in front of a cab. He hadn't been trampled by the home-going office workers, either. Perhaps his luck was changing.

He went down the steps, keeping a tight grip on the handrail. People pushed past him impatiently. Some gave him dirty looks. No one gave him a look of sympathy for his injured foot. New Yorkers!

He took a token out of his pocket with his free hand and managed to get through the turnstile without a problem. Then he had to walk down another long flight of steps to the passenger platform. The first train to stop was a local. He would have preferred an express, but he didn't want to wait.

The train had a few vacant seats. He boarded it and captured one for himself. Then he settled back for the long ride to Queens. The express wouldn't have stopped at every station as the local did, but at least he had a seat.

When the train finally reached his station, he got off and limped to a nearby bus stop. He had to wait, leaning on his crutch, for more than ten minutes before his bus showed up. When it did, he took a seat near the door.

He didn't have far to go, but it was already dusk. It seemed to him that the switch back to standard time had taken away more than an hour of daylight. It would be dark before he got inside his house.

The streetlights came on as he was climbing down to the sidewalk. He still had three blocks to go, but he felt better now. His mood always improved once he was in his own neighborhood. He had grown up in this area, lived his entire life in the same house, and knew almost everyone. They all called him Billy, even the newspaper boy.

Billy turned into a treelined street. The streetlight in front of his house and the next light down were both out. The line of trees turned the street into a long, dark tunnel. He was going to have to call whomever you called about such things. There was little enough light under the best of conditions. Now, with the lights out, half the block was in deep shadow.

He took a firm grip on his crutch and limped toward the house. It was the fourth one on the right. Billy lived in one half of a duplex—two separate homes that shared a central wall between them. All of the other houses on that side of the street had been put up by the same builder and followed the same design. The building trim and landscaping differed a bit, but they were all basically the same.

All of the houses seemed neat and well kept, except Number 374, Billy Mason's address. The plot of grass in front was a weed patch. The half of the duplex he owned hadn't been painted in 15 years. The dark, dusty drapes covering the windows made it look vacant, perhaps abandoned. He liked it that way. No one ever bothered him while he was working during the day or watching TV at night.

Billy dug out his keys and found the right one by touch. Nearing his walk, he noticed a strange car parked on the street in front of the building. "It must be someone visiting the Castles," he figured. They were the elderly couple who lived in the other half of his duplex.

The car was dark blue, and someone was in it. He saw a flare of light as a cigarette was lit. Then an arm appeared at the open window and pitched the match away. Whoever it was must be waiting for the Castles to come home, he thought.

At his walkway he looked at the car a bit more closely. It carried blue and white Washington, D.C., license plates. He couldn't remember the Castles having a visitor from D.C. before.

He limped up his walk, put the key in the lock, and hurried inside. Then he relocked the door and put on the chain. He moved through the house, turning on a small light in each room as he passed.

In the kitchen, he made himself a cup of instant coffee and sat down to drink it. It had been a long day for him. He had been on the go since 9:00 A.M., when he had twisted his ankle leaving the house. By noon it had hurt too much to walk on. He'd spent the rest of the afternoon finding a doctor.

Billy wondered what kind of day the rest of the world had enjoyed. He limped into the living room and turned on the TV to watch the news. It turned out the world was full of people who were a lot worse off than he was. The big stories concerned a plane crash in Spain and the FBI's arrest the night before of a Soviet spy.

Then he heard a sound from the back-yard he shared with his neighbors. It was the Castles' dog, Brutus, barking and running around. The Castles often left him loose to wander around in the backyard and on the walkway on their side of the duplex.

Brutus was a huge black animal of uncertain heritage. In the seven years the Castles had lived next door, the dog had never let Billy touch him. If Billy or anyone else came within a few feet of the animal, it showed its long white teeth.

"That dog's a killer," Billy once said.

"Nonsense," Mr. Castle said mildly. "Brutus likes people."

"Then I wish he wouldn't smile at me," Billy said, pointing at the dog's fangs. "If he *likes* people, it must be because he thinks they taste good."

Mr. Castle laughed quietly and reached over to pat the dog's head. He didn't have to reach down to do it. "Oh, Billy, you're always joking," the old man said.

Because Billy was a comedy writer, people seemed to think he was always joking. They didn't realize that being funny was a serious business. Humor was one thing he never wasted.

He heard a car door slam and went to the front window. As he pushed the drape aside, he wondered why he was feeling so uneasy. He never paid any attention to sounds from outside. Did he expect something to happen? But what?

The street seemed even darker than when he had come home. And the strange car was still there. It must have been its door he'd heard slam. A tall man, hardly more than a black shape, stood beside the car in deep shadow, waiting.

Waiting for what? Billy looked down the street but could see nothing. Then he looked in the direction of the nearest bus stop. Mr. and Mrs. Castle were coming slowly down the sidewalk with the light from the only working streetlight on them. The frail old couple seemed to cling to each other for warmth, or protection, as they walked.

Billy glanced at his watch—almost seven o'clock. That was right. If the couple went anywhere during the day, they almost always were home by seven. In the years they had lived next door to him, the Castles had never gone anywhere at night.

When the old couple reached their front walk, the tall man stepped out of the shadows and approached them. He towered over Mr. Castle. Two more large men stepped out from behind two trees in back of the Castles. The street was so dark Billy hadn't seen them. The first stranger waved a hand as though he were speaking. Then he struck the old man, knocking him to the pavement. The other two grabbed the woman from behind.

Billy had seen enough. He turned from the window and limped quickly into the kitchen where the telephone was located. He dialed 911.

"There's a mugging in progress," Billy said as soon as the emergency operator came on the line. "Right in front of my house—374 Marriot Place, Middle Village."

"Your name, sir?"

"Mason. Billy Mason."

"And your telephone number?"

Billy gave it to him. Then he hung up before the operator asked more useless questions. Billy hurried back to the window.

The street was quiet. There wasn't a sign of movement anywhere. And the strange car was gone.

The police arrived moments later. A cruiser pulled up with its red light flashing, and two officers jumped out. They ran to a pair of dark mounds lying on the grass plot between the sidewalk and the curb in front of the house. The

beam of one officer's flashlight revealed
the bodies of two men. Both had long dark
hair.

Two men? What happened to the Castles?

Billy went to the door, fumbled as he
unlocked it, and rushed outside.

"Are you the man who called?" one of
the officers asked.

"Yes," Billy answered, taking in the
scene. "Are they . . . are they dead?"

"Afraid so," the officer said. "Did you see
who did it?"

Confused, Billy looked from the bodies
on the ground to the lighted front window
of the Castles' house and back again.

"Er . . . perhaps . . . ," Billy offered.

"Maybe you'd better tell us what you
saw that made you call the police."

Billy told the policeman about the strange car and the man who had been waiting inside it. He also told them about the Castles coming home and the two other men who had attacked the couple. "When the man knocked Mr. Castle down, I left the window to call the emergency number."

"So that's the last thing you saw? You didn't see anything after that?"

"No. I was on the phone."

The officer nodded. He pointed to the bodies on the ground. "Okay, which of these men is Mr. Castle?"

"Neither one. I never saw them before. They must be two of the strangers."

"You said you saw the strangers."

"Sure, but . . . it was kind of dark. All I saw was their shapes."

They all looked toward the front of the Castles' house at the same time. A shadow passed on the other side of the drawn curtains. A rather small shadow.

"Maybe we can get some answers there," the officer said. He led the way to the front door and rang the bell.

Mrs. Castle answered the door, wearing her housecoat and slippers. She smiled at the policemen and ignored Billy. "Yes? Can I help you?"

"There are two dead men lying in front of your house. What can you tell us about it?"

The old woman's pale blue eyes seemed to grow larger. "Come inside," she said, stepping back.

"Better call this in," the officer told his partner before going inside. Billy followed him into the living room, looking around nervously for Brutus, the dog.

The policeman noticed Billy's hesitation. "What's wrong?" he asked.

"They have a mean dog that doesn't like people."

There was no sign of a dog anywhere. "Where's the dog, Mrs. Castle?" the officer asked.

"We don't have a dog," she told him.

The officer gave Billy a doubtful look. Then he turned back to the woman. "What happened out there?"

Mrs. Castle shook her head. "I have no idea. I've been watching television all evening. I didn't hear a thing."

"You've been in the house? You haven't been outside?"

"That's right."

"May I speak to your husband?"

"He isn't in," the old woman said. "He should be home soon, though. He ran out of pipe tobacco and went to buy some."

Billy went back outside with the policeman. Additional police had arrived and more were arriving. The street was taking on a circus atmosphere. A group of neighbors were standing around. Some were merely watching, while others tried to get into the act.

"I've seen a lot of strangers around here the last few days," Billy heard one of the neighbors say. It was Mr. Kytell, who lived across the street. He wore thick glasses that made his eyes look wide and frightened. His world was full of strangers. A friend more than 15 feet away looked like a stranger to him.

Two plainclothes detectives escorted Billy back to his house. He had to tell his story all over again to them.

One left to talk to Mrs. Castle. When he came back he wasn't very friendly.

"What makes you think you saw the Castles out on the sidewalk? It was too dark to identify the other men."

"I don't know," Billy said lamely. "I just did."

"Maybe you just thought it was the Castles because you expected to see them. That's possible, isn't it?"

"Well, maybe . . ."

"The medical examiner gave us an early report before the bodies were taken away. Whoever killed those men didn't use a weapon. The killer has to be some kind of martial arts expert. Do you have any reason to think either Mr. or Mrs. Castle is another Bruce Lee?"

"No, I don't," Billy said. He was beginning to feel foolish.

"Neither do I," the detective replied. "Mr. Castle returned from the store while I was talking to his wife. I think that little old man would need a weapon to kill a moth."

The detectives were finished with Billy. But it was another half hour before the police left and the street quieted down.

"How could I have made such a mistake?" Billy thought. "I could have sworn . . ." He shook his head.

This was crazy! They had him doubting his own eyes. Well, he didn't doubt them. He knew what he had seen. Mr. and Mrs. Castle had been attacked. He had missed what happened next, but he was certain that they had been involved.

Why would they lie about it? Even if they had killed the two men—though he couldn't imagine how—it had been in self-defense. The Castles didn't have anything to fear from the police.

Or did they?

And what happened to the third man and the car with the Washington, D.C., license plates? And where did Mr. Castle go so suddenly?

If Billy could find out the answers to any of these questions, he might be able to answer others, too. He limped over to the wall he shared with the Castles and pressed his ear against it. He couldn't hear a sound, not even their television. He wished he hadn't always been such a good neighbor. It was hard for him to spy on people he had treated with such respect.

Then he remembered the upstairs rear bedroom. That had been his room when he was growing up. When the windows were open, it was sometimes possible to hear what was said next door. Even though this was October, it was a warm night. They might have their windows open. It was worth a try.

Billy climbed the stairs to the second floor. He went into the rear bedroom and opened the window several inches. He listened, straining to hear any sound. Again, no luck.

He was about to leave the window when he heard Mrs. Castle speak. Her voice was sharp and clear, as though she were in the room with him. But Billy couldn't understand a word she said. She was speaking in some foreign language.

Mr. Castle broke in. "Speak English. How many times must I tell you? Always English. It must be a habit you never break."

"Even now?"

"Especially now. Our world is crumbling around us. Our training and discipline can save us, but we must not panic."

"Can't we get help?"

"I tried. I called the emergency number. Bornoff wasn't in his office. He won't be back until tomorrow afternoon. All I could do was leave a coded distress message and our code name."

"Isn't there anyone else you can contact?"

"No. Only Bornoff. I've always worked through him. He will have a safe house for us, new identity papers, and an escape route if we need it. But he must be able to find us. It will be best if we avoid involvement with the police."

"Bornoff?" Billy thought. That sounded like a Russian name. And the language Mrs. Castle was speaking—that could have been Russian, too. But that meant the Castles were . . . *spies*? Billy couldn't believe it.

"What about *him*?" Mrs. Castle asked. It wasn't clear to Billy who "him" was.

"We will take care of him tonight," Mr. Castle answered.

Had Mrs. Castle been pointing at Billy's house when she'd asked the question? Could they be talking about him, Billy wondered. A cold chill crept up his back despite the warm breeze at the window.

Billy stood listening for a long while but could make out only a few more words, never a complete sentence. The words he did hear weren't very comforting: "Body . . . blood . . . dead . . ." Any way you looked at those words, they didn't sound good.

It was after 11:00 when he heard the Castles' rear door open and close. Sounds of activity in the backyard followed. Billy looked out the window but could see nothing. Whatever the Castles were doing, they were too close to the building for him to see.

Billy gripped the bottom of the window and eased it farther up. He wanted room to stick his head out and see what was going on. When he figured he had enough space, he dropped to his knees and looked down into the Castles' half of the yard.

Moonlight brightened the scene. The old couple were digging in the flower bed next to their house. The soil must have been very soft because the hole was already a couple of feet wide and several feet long. Mr. Castle stood in the hole and was visible only from the waist up.

"What could they be looking for?" Billy wondered.

As he watched, the Castles went back into the house. They returned to view a few minutes later. They came out the door, carrying something heavy wrapped in a blue blanket. When the bundle was lying beside the hole, Billy could see a shoe sticking out of one end.

"Holy cow, they're digging a grave!" Now Billy knew what must have happened to the third man. He was killed, too, and the Castles had hidden his body in the house. Mrs. Castle was probably supposed to bring the others inside, too, while her husband got rid of the car. If the police hadn't arrived as quickly as they had, she probably would have done it.

Billy moved away from the window, his mind racing. The Castles were trying to get rid of the evidence. From what he'd over-heard earlier, they were planning an escape as soon as help arrived. If they could remain free until the following afternoon, they would succeed. He had to do something.

He limped downstairs, trying to ignore the pain in his ankle. He had to notify the police. He couldn't stop them by himself. They had killed three healthy men without using weapons. What chance could he have against them?

He dialed the police emergency number and told the operator who and where he was, and that he had a murder to report. He asked her to send someone right away. "But please, tell them not to use flashing lights or sirens. That might scare them away." Then he went outside to wait.

The uniformed officers who arrived were the same two who had answered his earlier call.

"Mr. and Mrs. Castle just dug a grave in their backyard," Billy told the older one. "I watched them drag a dead man's body outside. Then I called 911."

The policemen exchanged looks but didn't say anything.

Billy continued: "Remember, when I talked to you before? I said I'd seen three men attack the Castles. But only two bodies were out here. This must be the third man. They must have killed all three of them."

"Why do you think they did that?" the young officer asked in a quiet tone.

"Because they're spies. That car I saw earlier had Washington, D.C., license plates.

Government agents must have come to arrest them, but the Castles killed them."

The policemen exchanged looks again. The older one shrugged. "Might as well call for a backup," he told his partner. "There's probably nothing to it, but you never know."

Then to Billy he said, "You didn't say anything about Washington, D.C., license plates before. Why not?"

"I guess I forgot," Billy said.

"Forgot," the policeman echoed. "Right. People do that a lot. Especially if they've been drinking. You haven't been drinking, have you?"

"No," Billy answered, speaking with great care. "I haven't been drinking."

"You're walking kind of funny."

"I hurt my ankle."

"Uh-huh. Hurt your ankle." He didn't sound as though he believed a word Billy said.

Another police cruiser arrived. The older officer went over to explain the situation. He spoke in low tones Billy couldn't over-hear.

Finally, he returned. "We're going to drive around to the rear and take a look. Hop into the car," he said.

His partner took the wheel as Billy got into the backseat. They drove to the end of the block, turned left, and entered the alley that ran behind the houses.

The alley was even darker than the street in front. There were no lights for its entire length. Many of the backyards had trees that overhung the alley, making it as dark as a cave in some places.

The rear yard of the building Billy shared with the Castles was enclosed by a four-foot wooden fence. The officer stopped the car opposite the gate, and they all got out. The policemen let Billy lead the way through the gate. Then they followed with their flashlights pointing ahead of them toward the house.

They were just in time to catch Mr. Castle adding a last shovelful of earth to a mound against the building. His wife stood to one side, watching. The old couple turned quickly, but that was all the surprise they showed.

"Is something wrong, officers?" Mrs. Castle asked calmly.

Billy's story seemed less ridiculous in view of the mound of earth. The older officer seemed a little shocked, but he recovered quickly. "That's what we're here to find out," he said. He glanced at Billy. "We've had a report you folks were burying a body out here." He casually rested his right hand on the butt of his pistol.

Mrs. Castle laughed lightly. "That's silly," she said.

"Perhaps," the policeman agreed. "But would you mind telling me what you're doing out here? It's nearly midnight. Not a normal hour for yard work."

"No, it isn't," Mr. Castle said. "We had planned to do this earlier today, but several things came up." He began rubbing his feet on the grass to scrape the mud from his shoes.

"Do what?"

"Bury our dog. He died, and we buried him," Mr. Castle said mildly.

The officer took a step backward and seemed to stand straighter. "When I spoke to your wife earlier, she told me you didn't have a dog."

"Well, that was true. Poor old Brutus was already dead," he said sadly. Then he turned to Billy. "This is hardly the time for one of your jokes," he accused.

"Jokes?" the officer asked.

Mr. Castle said, "Mr. Mason is a comedy writer. Sometimes he gets carried away, or at least his imagination does."

"Is that true?" the policeman asked Billy.

"The part about me being a comedy writer is true. The rest isn't. I saw them bury a man, not a dog."

"Are you sure this isn't some kind of joke?" the officer asked.

"Did the two men you found earlier look like a joke?" Billy asked.

The officer thought about that for a moment. "Mr. Castle," he said, "there's a way we can settle this quickly."

"What's that?"

"With your permission, we can open that mound and take a look," the officer said.

"Oh, no!" Mrs. Castle protested. "I'd rather you didn't do that."

"I don't think there's any other way," the officer said reasonably. "You can see how serious this looks. We can't just walk away. Either you let us check the mound now, or we'll do it later with a court order. You won't have us out of your hair until we do."

"In that case," the old man said, "go ahead and look. But please don't make more of a mess than necessary. We were very fond of Brutus. We don't like having him disturbed this way."

The officer nodded to his partner who then picked up the shovel that was leaning against the house. He went to the mound and worked quickly. About a foot down, the shovel struck something soft, and he began to dig more carefully. Soon a section of blue blanket was exposed.

"That's the blanket they dragged the body out in," Billy said. No one looked at him. The blanket had everyone's attention.

The policeman was on his knees now, clearing dirt away with his hands. One end of the blanket was uncovered. He pulled it open to show the head of a large black dog. In death, Brutus looked no more peaceful than he had in life.

"All right, cover him up again," the officer said. "Mr. Mason was seeing things."

The officer looked at the Castles. "We're sorry about this," he said. "It looks as if this is just what you said it was. But I'd double-check with the Board of Health about burying your dog in your backyard. There may be some rule against it."

The Castles nodded and smiled.

Turning to Billy, the officer said, "I think you owe these people an apology."

Billy turned red, mumbled, "Sorry," and fled into his house through the rear door. A few minutes later, he heard the police leave.

Totally confused, Billy sat at the kitchen table, holding his head in his hands. How could he have been so wrong? He *had* seen a shoe sticking out of the end of that blanket. Brutus didn't wear shoes. The Castles *had* dragged a body from the house. He knew they had.

But what had happened to it?

Why hadn't the police found it in the grave?

Where was it now?

"Wait a minute. Slow down," he told himself. "There has to be a logical explanation for this."

He tried to make sense out of what he knew. Brutus was dead, and they'd buried him. How—and why? He thought about it for a moment. Well, the last time he'd heard the dog, it was out in the backyard. Suppose the dog had wandered around to the walkway at the side of the house. At the end of the walkway was a wooden gate leading to the sidewalk. It was often left unlocked. When the Castles were attacked, the dog could have pushed open the gate and charged out to help them. One of the agents could have shot the dog in self-defense.

Then, after the Castles somehow killed the three agents, they decided to get rid of the men and the dog to cover everything up. But the Castles had only enough time to drag the dog and one body inside. This all must have taken place while Billy was calling the police the first time.

When the police arrived, Mrs. Castle denied any knowledge of the two men on the sidewalk. The police left, but the Castles still had a dead dog and a dead man to get rid of.

But they had dug only one hole.

Of course! The Castles had buried them both in the same grave. That had to be the answer.

When Billy had seen Mr. Castle standing in the hole, the sides had been up to his waist. But when the policeman had uncovered the dog's body, he had had to dig down only about a foot. That proved there was something else in the grave.

Billy reached for the telephone but stopped with his hand outstretched. He had already brought out the police with one false alarm. They would be slow to act on another call from him. When he called, it would have to be with more than suspicions. He had to have proof—solid proof—that the Castles couldn't twist with clever lies.

Billy pressed his ear to the common wall, but he could hear nothing from the Castles' side. Had they gone to bed? Or, more likely, were they sitting quietly, waiting for their Russian friend to come? Billy had overheard the old man say that he expected help the following afternoon. It was already past 1:00 A.M. now. So, help wasn't many hours away.

Billy knew what he had to do, but he was forced to wait. He couldn't do anything until he was sure the Castles were in the front of their house. So he waited—through the night. From time to time, he approached the wall to listen, but he heard nothing. He drank several cups of coffee during the early morning to help him stay awake.

Shortly after dawn he heard the Castles' television. They had it tuned to an early morning news program. They were probably both watching it. That should give him the time he needed.

Billy took a shovel from his basement and went into the backyard. Working quietly, he dug down to the blue blanket that covered the dog. He gripped it with both hands and gave a mighty heave, pulling it out of the ground.

As he expected, the earth beneath it was loosely packed. He began to dig again. He pushed aside the soil until he found the blanket with the shoe sticking out of the end. He opened the blanket to confirm that there was a foot in the shoe and a leg attached to the foot. He wasn't willing to go any further than that.

He left everything where it was and went back to his house. Maybe now the police would listen—and believe him.

As he reached for the telephone, it began to ring. He grabbed the handset. "Hello," he said.

"Mr. Mason?"

"Yes," Billy said impatiently.

"My name is John Romane. I'm a government agent. I need your help." It was the voice of a man used to giving orders and having them obeyed.

"Yes," Billy said with more interest.

"Your neighbors are an elderly couple named Castle." It wasn't a question.

"Yes," Billy said for the third time.

"They are very dangerous people."

"Yes," Billy agreed.

"Do you know if they are at home?"

"I think so. They were a few minutes ago." At last he was able to give a longer-than-one-word answer.

"Good," Romane said. "I want you to go to their front door and ring the bell. Ignore the two men you will see hiding beside the entrance. Tell the Castles you want to talk to them about something. They know you. They will unlock the door for you. Leave the rest to us."

"Okay," Billy agreed, hanging up the phone.

He found his crutch and used it to take some of the weight off his ankle. He had already done too much walking without it. Then he left his house and limped to the Castles' front door.

There were two men, one standing on each side of the entrance. Their bodies were pressed against the building. Each had a large black pistol in his hand. Not looking at them was the hardest thing Billy had ever done.

He pushed the doorbell, waited about half a second, then pushed it again. What if they wouldn't answer the door? He rang again.

The door didn't open, but Mr. Castle spoke from the inside. "Yes? Who is it?"

"Er . . . Billy Mason, Mr. Castle. I want to talk to you."

The door remained closed.

"What about?"

"Er . . . the grave in the backyard. I've been back there doing some digging. I found the body of the man you buried with Brutus. I thought you might like to talk about it before I call the police again."

That did the trick. "All right. Just a moment," the old man said.

There was the sound of a heavy metal bar being lifted. Then the door swung open. Billy saw Mr. Castle standing to one side of the door. His wife was across the room.

The men with guns brushed roughly past Billy and charged into the house. As the first one stepped through the doorway, he was kicked in the head by Mr. Castle. The man's head snapped back, and he dropped like a sack of potatoes falling off a loading dock.

The second man reacted quickly. He reached back and grabbed Billy by the sleeve. Then he swung Billy into the room ahead of him, pushing him into Mr. Castle. By the time they managed to untangle their arms, legs, and the crutch, the second agent's pistol was aimed at the old man's head.

Mrs. Castle started toward them from across the room. But she was stopped by a third man who entered. He, too, carried a large black pistol. "Stay where you are!" he ordered.

"Mr. Romane!" Billy said with relief. He recognized the voice from the telephone.

Romane took charge immediately. The Castles were forced to sit on the floor in the center of the room. Romane kept his weapon aimed at them while the other man looked after their fallen comrade. The man came to in a few minutes. But he had a broken nose to show for his contact with the old man's foot.

Then Romane noticed Billy. "Ah, Mr. Mason. I see you are still here," he said, as if Billy would leave with all that excitement going on.

"Yes, sir," Billy said. "Is there anything I can do?"

"Yes," he said, pointing his pistol at Billy's chest. "Sit on the floor with the Castles."

"But they're spies!" Billy protested.

"We are *all* spies, Mr. Mason. You are the only one who is not a spy."

"But . . . but you said you were a government agent," Billy said.

"That is true," Romane replied. His lips parted in a nasty smile that reminded Billy of the dog Brutus. "But I didn't say which government."

"**V**ery funny," Billy said in a flat tone as he sat down.

Billy looked at the Castles. They hadn't changed from the way they had always appeared. But Billy looked at them quite differently. After seeing the ease with which Mr. Castle had knocked out the armed man, Billy had no trouble thinking of the old man as dangerous. Very, very dangerous.

Now the old couple sat beside him on the floor without a sign of emotion. They seemed completely relaxed. They seemed alert to what was going on around them but showed no trace of fear or anger. It was as though they didn't have a care in the world.

Billy wasn't sure who was worse—the Castles or Romane's bunch. They were all scary.

It looked as if Romane intended to kill the Castles and Billy along with them. Billy didn't like that at all. To top it off, he still didn't know what was going on. His guesses had made sense only until he learned a new fact or something new happened. Then all his thinking had to be revised.

Surrounded by men with pistols, Billy thought his hours of playing detective had ended. If he were going to find out what was going on, someone would have to tell him.

"What's all this about?" he asked. "Who are you, anyway? I'll bet your name isn't John Romane."

The man smiled. "That's true. But it's close. It's Romanov—Ivan Romanov." Billy turned white when he realized what that meant. "And I thought you would have figured out what was going on by now. But I guess this must be confusing. The Castles here don't look like the spies you Americans imagine."

Billy rubbed his ankle. It was throbbing with pain from all the walking he had done without his crutch.

"You seem to have hurt your ankle, Mr. Mason. That's too bad." He paused and smiled. "I promise you, it won't hurt much longer," he added.

Romanov turned to the Castles. "You heard Mr. Mason. He is puzzled. He wants to know what all this is about. That seems like a reasonable request. Why don't you tell him? I, too, would like to hear your explanation."

The Castles ignored him.

"Not very cooperative, are they, Mr. Mason? It's difficult to believe that we are on the same side, isn't it? In fact, in view of recent events, I have serious doubts. Very serious doubts."

Romanov towered over them, smiling like a man who knew he held all the cards— and they were aces. Whatever the game was, it was over. And Romanov had won.

"Mr. Mason, do you know what a sleeper is? No? A sleeper is an agent sent to a foreign country long before anyone thinks he or she will be needed. Mr. and Mrs. Castle are sleepers. My government sent them here 30 years ago. They assumed the identities of a couple who had been killed in an auto accident. For 30 years they lived normal lives. They were never needed.

"However, when they were finally called upon to serve their country, their work was very poor. Information they gathered was either of little value or not very accurate. We began to wonder whether they were working for our government or yours. Double agents are common.

"It was decided to send them home for . . . er . . . questioning. Because of our suspicions, we had to have a good excuse, or we'd risk frightening them. They had to think the trip was merely a routine step we were taking for their safety.

"Two days ago one of our other agents was arrested. That gave us the excuse we needed. The Castles were notified that the arrested agent might talk and give their names. For their protection, we were flying them back to their homeland.

"Yesterday, three men were sent here. They never returned. Last night, the television news told of two dead men found in front of this house. It was clear the Castles had resisted the men sent to collect them. It was also clear your FBI wasn't involved. If it were, I don't think there would have been anything in the news. The Castles have simply lived in this country too long. They think of it as their home and don't want to work against it."

Billy nodded. That all fit. Except for one thing. "Who is Bornoff?" he asked.

The old man's head swung around and his eyes narrowed. Billy knew he had made another blunder.

"Where did you hear that name?" Romanov asked, leaning forward with interest.

"Er . . . yesterday, before the killings," Billy lied. "A man tried to sell me some fire insurance. He said his name was Bornoff. I thought he was involved, but I guess I was wrong."

Romanov laughed. "You Americans are so stupid. Even when you have all the pieces, you can never put a puzzle together. Ex-comrade Bornoff 'turned' about 15 years ago. He's now an agent for your government. He's probably a contact for our friends here." He nodded toward the Castles. "Well, it doesn't really matter, anyway."

He took a pair of handcuffs out of his pocket and tossed them onto the rug in front of the old man. He ordered him to cuff his right wrist to his wife's left one. Then he had Billy squeeze the steel loops to be certain they were tightly closed.

"We are going to take a little ride," Romanov announced. "There is a plane waiting for us at a small private field on Long Island. Our car is at the curb."

Billy and the Castles were marched quickly outside. The Castles were placed in the car's rear seat while Billy leaned on his crutch and waited his turn.

Suddenly, Romanov said something in a foreign language. His tone was angry. He switched back to English and it became clear. He had discovered that two of the sedan's tires were flat. They weren't going anywhere in that car.

As Romanov tried to decide what to do, a service station tow truck came slowly down the street. He saw it and smiled. He and his men quickly put their weapons away. Romanov stepped off the curb and held up his hand to stop the truck. Two men wearing gray coveralls sat in the cab.

"Can you fix a couple of flats for me?" Romanov asked, waving a large bill.

"Sure, buddy," one of the men said. They climbed down and followed him to the car.

No one was paying much attention to Billy. So he picked up his crutch and hit the nearest spy over the head with it. When the other two turned on him, the mechanics stuck guns into their backs.

"FBI! Don't move! You're under arrest!"

Suddenly, more FBI men appeared. The Castles were released, and Romanov and his men were taken away. It was over that quickly.

Two flat tires and a convenient tow truck. Billy had known that was too good to be true, even if Romanov hadn't.

One of the men in coveralls was in charge of the FBI team. He put his hand on Billy's shoulder. "I suppose you want to know what this is all about?" he said. "I'm sorry, but I can't tell you, even though you helped us make this arrest."

"No need to be sorry," Billy said. "I know what was going on. The Castles were working for you and didn't want to return to their own country. You must have called your office, received their message, and known they were in trouble. That's right, isn't it, Agent Bornoff?"

"Say, how do you know my name?" the man said in surprise.

Billy smiled. After being in the dark for so long, it felt good to be one step ahead for a change.

"That's my little secret," Billy said.